Dragons Don't Throw Snowballs

by **Debbie Dadey**
and
Marcia Thornton Jones

illustrated by John Steven Gurney

A
LITTLE APPLE
PAPERBACK

SCHOLASTIC INC.
New York Toronto London Auckland Sydney
Mexico City New Delhi Hong Kong Buenos Aires

For Katherine, Erhin, and Ryan Kasun
—DD

To Joanne Nicoll:
A "treasure" of a friend!
—MTJ

ISBN 0-439-79337-8

12 11 10 9

17 18 19 20/0
40

Printed in the U.S.A.
First Scholastic printing, March 2006

Contents

1

Snow, Snow, and MORE Snow!

"This is crazy," Melody told her best friend, Liza.

The girls waited under a giant snow-laden oak tree for Howie and Eddie. A blanket of white covered the surrounding playground. Icicles dangled from the roof of Bailey Elementary School. The girls' breath hung in clouds when they spoke.

Melody knocked snowflakes off her black braids. "I like snow as much as any kid, but we have too much. Mom won't drive anywhere because of it. I've never seen so much snow in my life."

"Snow can be nice," Liza said softly. "It makes everything look like it's covered in marshmallow cream."

"But the best thing about snow is the Winter Carnival," Melody said. "Now that it's over the snow has turned to slush."

Bailey City held a Winter Carnival every year complete with a parade and a snow-sculpture contest. It was something the kids in town loved.

Liza sighed. "Maybe you're right. Even the winning snow sculpture looks sad." She pointed to the yard across the street.

A man named Dr. Victor rented one of the houses next to the school. The girls knew he ran the Shelley Science Museum outside of town. Some kids even thought Dr. Victor was a mad scientist trying to make a Frankenstein monster. They almost never saw Dr. Victor because he spent long hours at the museum.

"Who would've guessed that Dr. Victor liked playing in the snow," Melody said.

The two girls remembered the day before the carnival when Dr. Victor had rolled giant snowballs to form the lumpy spine of a snow dragon with a long, curling tail. The dragon had been sparkling white for the contest. Now the snow was dirty, making the sculpture's eyes an angry gray and the scales seem dark and gloomy. The dragon looked like it was ready to leap into the air and attack.

"It's hard to believe that it's made out of snow," Liza said. "It looks so real."

"I think it looks bored," Melody said with a shrug. "Just like me and every other kid in Bailey City."

"I wonder if real dragons get bored sleeping in their caves while they protect their treasure," Liza wondered out loud.

"What treasure?" Melody asked.

Liza rolled her eyes. "Everyone knows that dragons hoard treasure. They keep it in caves and they curl around the treasure to protect it."

Melody laughed. "Those are just stories. Dragons can't get bored because they aren't real. But I AM bored. I'm bored with winter, cold weather, and this snow, snow, SNOW!"

"Snow is fun," Liza said. "We can build snowmen and snow forts."

"We don't have time for that," Melody said as she pushed up her coat sleeve to look at her watch. "We have to get to school. We're going to be late if Howie and Eddie don't hurry. Do you see them anywhere?"

Liza glanced across the street. A flicker of movement caught her eye. "Did you see that?" she shrieked. "The dragon just winked at me!"

2

Snow Battle

Pow!

A snowball thumped into Melody's stomach. She doubled over to catch her breath.

Bam!

Another one crashed into Liza's shoulder. L a teetered off balance and sat down hard in the snow.

"Help! Help! We're being attacked by dragons!" Liza screamed.

"It's worse than dragons!" Melody said, ducking for cover behind the oak tree's trunk. "It's BOYS!"

Sure enough, Eddie and Howie jumped up from behind the dragon. They looked both ways and raced across the street.

"You're going to pay for that!" Melody yelled.

Eddie shoved his ball cap over his red hair and got ready for battle. "We'd like to see you try!"

"You'll never beat us!" Howie added. The boys lobbed snowball after snowball before the girls could make a single one.

"After them!" Melody yelled to Liza, reaching down to grab a handful of snow.

"NO!" Liza yelled. "We'll get our school clothes all wet."

Melody didn't listen. She wasn't about to let Howie and Eddie win this snow battle. Besides, she wanted to have a little fun.

To get a good shot at the boys, Melody had to get closer. She darted across the playground. She dodged behind the Dumpster. Then she slid behind a parked car. "Get them!" Melody screamed as she hurried to form snowballs.

Eddie's red hair made a great target. At least two of Melody's snowballs smashed into his ball cap, but her few snowballs were no match for Eddie and Howie's arsenal. They must've been hiding behind the dragon for a long time, filling their coat pockets with snowball after snowball.

Liza ducked behind the oak tree's trunk, but no matter where she moved, the boys' snowballs found their mark. They thumped into her stomach, back, and legs as she raced toward the Dumpster.

"Get her!" Eddie hollered as Liza made a break for the school doors.

When the boys reached the playground, they grabbed more snow. Snowballs sailed after Liza like hawks zeroing in on a helpless mouse.

Liza slipped on a slick patch of ice. Down she went. She covered her head as snowballs fell to the ground all around her.

Plop!
Plop!
Plop!

"Help me! Help me!" Liza shrieked like a damsel in distress.

No sooner were the words out of her mouth than a deep rumble shook the ground. A giant cloud blocked out the sun and coated the snow in shadows.

Melody tripped on her shoelace and got a face full of snow.

Howie ducked.

Eddie started to look up. He never got a chance because just then, a mound of snow dropped out of the sky and fell right on the two boys' heads.

3

Let It Snow!

"Did you hear that?" Liza asked.

"Was it a plane?" Melody asked. "Was it a garbage truck?"

"Maybe it was an asteroid," Liza suggested. She shook her blond hair and snow flew off her ponytail.

"It was an earthquake!" Eddie said when he popped up out of the snow.

Howie brushed the snow off his head. "Don't be silly. It was probably just thunder."

"In the dead of winter?" Liza asked. "In a snowstorm?"

Howie shrugged. "On rare occasions, conditions can be right for winter thunder." Howie's dad was a scientist so Howie knew things like that.

Eddie looked around the playground

and made a fist. "I don't care about a silly rumble of thunder. I care about revenge! I want to find out who threw that giant snowball."

"Nobody could make a snowball that size," Howie said, pointing to the broken mound of snow at Eddie's feet.

"Then what threw it?" Eddie said, putting his snow-covered gloves on his hips. "And don't give me that rot about thunder."

Melody giggled. "It was probably just perfect timing for snow to fall from the top of the oak tree."

Eddie didn't look convinced. "If you're wrong, that means someone has it out for me. I intend to find whoever it is!"

"Melody's right," Howie said. "I'm sure it's nothing to worry about. But this snow is!"

Even bigger flakes had started falling from the sky. "Oh, no," Melody groaned. "Snow, snow, and more snow. I'm sick of it!"

"Maybe we'll have a snow day!" Eddie said cheerfully. "No more pencils. No more books. No more teachers' dirty looks. Snow day! Snow day! Snow day!"

Melody laughed, too. She wouldn't mind a few days off from homework. "In that case, all I can say is let it snow."

Liza giggled and put her head beside Melody's. The two friends sang, "Let it snow! Let it snow! Let it snow!"

Eddie rolled his eyes. He didn't care about singing, but he did love snow days. In fact, he loved any day without school. While the girls were singing, Eddie glanced around the playground. He wanted to make sure that no one was hiding out. Someone like Ben, the fourth-grade bully, who liked to tease Eddie. It'd be just like Ben to heave a big blob of snow like that. But the playground was eerily quiet. So quiet, Eddie felt like he could hear the snow dragon next door breathing.

Before the door to Bailey School closed with a thud behind the four friends, Liza looked across the street. She blinked. Once inside, she used her mitten to rub a clear spot in the door's window.

The snow dragon was gone!

4

Ice Tricks

"Your eyes were playing tricks on you," Melody told Liza after they had hung up their coats. "That dragon is nothing but snow and ice. It can't move."

Liza was not convinced. She could barely keep her mind on writing her English sentences. Twice she forgot to start with a capital letter. Her eyes kept drifting to the window, but the yard with the dragon couldn't be seen from her classroom.

Finally, Liza could stand it no longer. She tore a tiny piece of paper from the corner of her spelling worksheet and wrote a note.

Liza held up her hand. "May I please go to the bathroom?" she asked Mrs.

Jeepers. Liza's voice shook a little. Her teacher scared her. Some kids at Bailey Elementary believed their third-grade teacher was a vampire. After all, she came from Transylvania and lived in a haunted house. Even worse, Mrs. Jeepers wore a mysterious brooch every day. When the kids forgot to behave, their teacher had a habit of rubbing the green stone on her brooch. That was never a good thing because the kids were pretty sure the pin was magic and made them behave.

Mrs. Jeepers flashed her eyes in Liza's direction, but then nodded. As Liza walked down the aisle, she dropped the note on Melody's desk. *Meet me in the hall*, it said.

Liza had to wait a full three minutes before her friend appeared in the hallway. "This better be good," Melody said. "Mrs. Jeepers didn't look like she believed I had to go to the bathroom, too. I had to jump up and down and do the potty dance. Eddie laughed at me."

Liza pulled her friend toward the outside doors. "That dragon was gone," she said. "I'm sure of it, and I'm going to prove it."

Melody rolled her eyes. "Not this again," she said, but she followed Liza to the door that led to the playground.

Liza rubbed a clear circle in the foggy window and then stepped aside so her friend could look. "Well?" Liza asked as

Melody pressed her nose to the glass. "What do you see?"

The snow was falling faster than before. The flakes weren't as big, but so much was coming down it looked like a dizzy curtain of white. Melody was quiet for a moment. Then she turned to look at Liza. "What I see is a dragon," Melody said, "made of ice and snow. Now can we please go back to class before Mrs. Jeepers realizes we're not where we're supposed to be?" Melody took off down the hall without waiting for Liza to answer.

Liza shivered from the cold coming through the glass as she looked out the window. It was hard to see through the falling snow, but she had to admit Melody was right. The snow-sculpture dragon was back on the lawn, only this time Liza thought he smiled at her.

5

Snow Disaster

By lunchtime, the snow was falling so fast that the kids couldn't see out the windows. A vicious wind whipped around the building, swirling the snow into drifts so high a camel would be lost in them.

"It's a blizzard," Melody said as they made their way back from the cafeteria after lunch with their class. The four friends were at the end of the line. They let the rest of the third-graders get ahead so they could talk.

Eddie nodded. "It's great," he said. "We won't have school for a week!"

Howie looked worried. "When will we work on our science experiments if they cancel school?"

"They'll have to call off the science projects, too," Eddie said. He looked like he was ready to cheer until he saw Howie's face. Howie loved science.

Liza patted Howie on the shoulder. "Don't worry about your project. I'm sure Mrs. Jeepers will give us extra time when we come back from the snow days. Besides, we have bigger things to worry about than science projects."

"Like what?" Melody asked.

"Dragons," Liza said.

Eddie jumped in front of Liza and thumped her on the forehead. "I just figured out what my science project will be. The study of a brainless third-grader named Liza!"

Melody giggled and even Howie smiled at Eddie's joke. Liza did not think it was funny at all.

"I know that snow dragon moved," she argued. She had been trying to convince her friends of what she had seen all during lunch, but no one believed her.

"The swirling snow played tricks on your eyes," Melody said for the umpteenth time

as the kids walked into their classroom. "Believe me, that dragon is nothing but a frozen lump of water."

Liza wanted to argue, but Mrs. Jeepers was waiting for them to start a new social studies unit. The kids sat down and opened their books, but it was hard to concentrate. Because of the snow, they were sure that they wouldn't have to worry about school for at least a week.

Their teacher was in the middle of showing the third-graders how to find latitude and longitude on a map when the intercom snapped, popped, and then squealed to life.

"May I have your attention, please?" Principal Davis's voice boomed.

Mrs. Jeepers flashed her eyes at the students until they all sat still and listened.

"The mayor has just made an emergency announcement," Principal Davis continued over the loudspeaker. "Because of record snowfall, all Bailey City roads are closed. Buses are stranded. Cars are unable to make it through the piling snowdrifts. It's official. Bailey City is shut down! Obviously, students can't walk home in this kind of blizzard. There's only one thing to do. All students must remain at school until the emergency is over. Your parents have been notified."

With that, the loudspeaker went dead.

Eddie jumped up and grabbed his chest. "No!" he gasped. "It can't be. Say it isn't so!"

Their teacher, Mrs. Jeepers, gently rubbed the mysterious brooch at her throat and flashed her green eyes in Eddie's direction.

Eddie immediately sat down.

"This is an extreme situation," Mrs. Jeepers explained. "But we will be safe spending the night right here in Bailey Elementary."

Most of the kids groaned. A couple

whimpered. A boy named Huey raised his hand. "What will we eat?"

Mrs. Jeepers looked at the students. Her tongue flitted out to lick her lips before she answered. "I am sure," she finally said, "there will be plenty of peanut butter and jelly sandwiches."

A girl named Carey batted her eyelashes at Eddie. It was a known fact that Carey didn't just like Eddie. She LIKED Eddie. "We're stranded! Right here! TOGETHER!" she said. "Isn't it romantic?"

Eddie looked like he might be sick at any minute. "Only if you think the end of the world is r-r-r . . ." Eddie couldn't bring himself to say "romantic." "That r-word," he said instead.

"It won't be so bad," Melody assured Eddie.

"What's the worst that could happen?" Liza added.

"Maybe it will be fun," Howie said. "We can play games and tell ghost stories."

Mrs. Jeepers cleared her throat to get the students' attention. "How wonderful," she said. "Now we have even more time to learn about longitude and latitude. After that we will begin our next mathematics unit on area and perimeter. And then we will . . ."

Obviously, the last thing Mrs. Jeepers had in mind was playing games or telling stories.

Eddie thunked his head on his desk. "This isn't a snow day," he groaned. "It's a snow DISASTER!"

6

WHOMP! WHOMP! SWOOSH!

The kids were exhausted by the time they ate dinner. Eddie had blisters on his fingers from doing so many math problems. The kids were so tired they could barely eat their peanut butter and jelly sandwiches. Even the sugar cookies were hard to swallow. "We're like Hansel and Gretel trapped in a witch's house," Eddie mumbled to his friends as Mrs. Jeepers led them to the gym.

"Only Mrs. Jeepers is no witch," Melody said. "She's a vampire."

"We can't sleep tonight," Liza whimpered. "We have to stay awake and make sure Mrs. Jeepers doesn't sprout fangs."

Melody looked at her teacher. "Did you notice that Mrs. Jeepers didn't eat a bite of her sandwich? She didn't even nibble her cookie. In fact, she didn't eat a thing."

Eddie nodded. "She's saving her appetite for something more to her liking," he said. "Blood. Ours!"

Liza whimpered. She sniffed. Liza's nose bled whenever she was really nervous. "I think my nose is going to bleed," she told her friends.

"NO!" Howie said. "Whatever you do, don't get a nosebleed. Vampires love nosebleeds."

"Take three deep breaths," Melody said. She waited while her friend breathed slowly. "We have to stay brave. That's the only way we'll make it through the night."

Liza nodded, but she didn't look very brave as the kids filed into the gym.

Big blue tumbling mats covered with blankets were spread across the floor. Televisions on tall stands stood in the four corners. The room was filled with kids from other classrooms.

"Let's make the best of a bad situation," Principal Davis said as he looked at the teachers and the students. "As soon as you are settled in for a long winter's night, we'll read stories and watch movies until bedtime!"

Several kids cheered. It would've sounded like fun if Liza didn't know that they were sharing the gym with a vampire.

The kids found mats near the back of the room. Once they were settled, they listened to story after story and watched movie after movie. One by one, the kids around them fell asleep. A few teachers wandered around the room to make sure everyone was settled before turning the lights down. Then even the teachers found a place to get comfortable. Everybody was falling asleep. Everyone, that is, except Liza.

She tossed. She turned. She flipped. She flopped.

Finally, Melody threw the blanket they were sharing to the side and sat up. Liza looked very small and pale on the blue tumbling mat.

"You're homesick," Melody said. "And so am I."

"Me, too," Howie whispered from the next mat over.

Eddie was sharing a mat with Howie. "It's hard to sleep when you think you're bat bait," Eddie admitted.

"I can't sleep for another reason," Liza whimpered.

"What could be worse than being homesick?" Howie asked.

"And vampires?" wondered Eddie.

"I'll tell you what," Liza told them as she sat up. "It's something big. Very big. And it's outside waiting for us!"

Eddie rubbed his eyes. "Duh!" he said. "It's called the biggest snowstorm in Bailey City history."

"I'm not talking about snow," she said.

"I'm talking about a living, breathing monster! A dragon!"

Melody, Howie, and Eddie all opened their mouths to argue, but Liza put up a hand to stop them. "You'll have to prove me wrong," Liza said.

"Fine," Eddie said. "Let's get this over with so we can get some sleep."

"There's no way we can get out of the gym," Howie hissed. "Have you forgotten that our teacher is a vampire? Vampires don't sleep."

Eddie glanced around the room. The dim emergency lamps cast a weak light over the sleeping students. It took him a while, but Eddie finally spotted Mrs. Jeepers. She sat in a chair, with her eyes closed, and a fat book in her lap. Her head tilted to one side.

"Could she really be asleep?" Melody asked.

"Vampires never sleep," Liza warned.

Before his friends could stop him, Eddie

started crawling along the outside of the room toward the doors. Liza looked at Melody. Melody glanced at Howie. Howie looked at Mrs. Jeepers. Their teacher let out a little snore.

"I guess our teacher is one vampire that DOES sleep," Howie said. Then he started crawling after Eddie. Melody and Liza waited for Mrs. Jeepers to let out another snore just to make sure she was sound asleep. Then they followed their two friends.

Once they escaped the gym, Liza took the lead. Long shadows followed them as they weaved through the twisted hallways. "What will you do if you find this legendary monster?" Eddie wanted to know.

Melody giggled. "We could feed it a midnight snack. Maybe there's some peanut butter left."

"I bet snow dragons would prefer an Eddie-sicle," Howie added as they made their way to the playground door.

"Very funny," Eddie snapped.

The window in the door was frosted with a thick layer of ice, so the kids couldn't see outside. Liza reached for the door to pull it open. Her fingers were inches from the door handle when she froze.

"Shhh." Liza held up her hand to silence her friends. "Did you hear that?"

Her friends stopped and held their breaths. That's when they heard exactly what Liza was talking about. It came from outside, and it sounded big. Very big.

Whomp. Whomp. Swoosh.

Whomp. Whomp. Swoosh.

Closer and closer it came. It was right outside the door.

WHOMP. WHOMP. SWOOSH.

WHOMP. WHOMP. SWOOSH.

"Run!" Liza screamed.

The kids dashed down the hall. They skidded around corners. They didn't stop until they reached the gym where the rest of their class was sacked out on blue mats.

Eddie didn't think twice about jumping

over sleeping kids. Melody didn't worry about being caught by Mrs. Jeepers. Howie didn't try to be quiet. They all made a mad dash for their mats and dived under their blankets.

Liza pulled the blanket over her head. Then she heard the noise again.

Whomp. Whomp. Swoosh.

Whomp. Whomp. Swoosh.

Whatever was making that sound had followed the kids all the way to this side of the building.

WHOMP. WHOMP. SWOOSH.

"It's going to fly through the ceiling and get us," Liza whimpered. She did the only thing she could think of.

Liza squeezed her eyes shut and waited for the dragon to attack.

7

Snoring Vampires

The next thing Liza knew, it was morning. She had fallen asleep waiting for the dragon to attack. All around the gym were lumps of sleeping children under blankets. "Are you awake?" Liza whispered to Melody.

Melody peeked from under the red blanket and yawned. "I had this crazy dream that a monster was trying to get inside the school."

Liza knew exactly what Melody had heard. Liza spoke quietly so she wouldn't wake the other kids. "That wasn't a dream. It was the sound of real dragon wings."

"Whatever it was," Melody said, "it sure made a strange noise."

Eddie crawled up between Melody and

Liza. "I thought about it last night. I bet that noise was just a snowplow clearing the playground," he said.

"I've never heard a snowplow sound like that," Liza said.

"I know how to find out for sure," Howie told them as he crawled up behind Eddie. "All we have to do is check out the tracks made in the snow."

Eddie grinned. Nothing made him happier than sneaking around like a spy. He scrambled toward the door, going from sleeping kid to sleeping kid and keeping as far from Mrs. Jeepers as possible. She sat in a chair, snoring.

Liza giggled softly. "Who knew that vampires snored?"

"Let's get out of here before she wakes up," Melody warned. "Besides, I have to go the bathroom." The kids crept out of the room and into the hallway.

Melody made a pit stop at the bathroom and then the kids looked out the window by the cafeteria. "There are tracks,

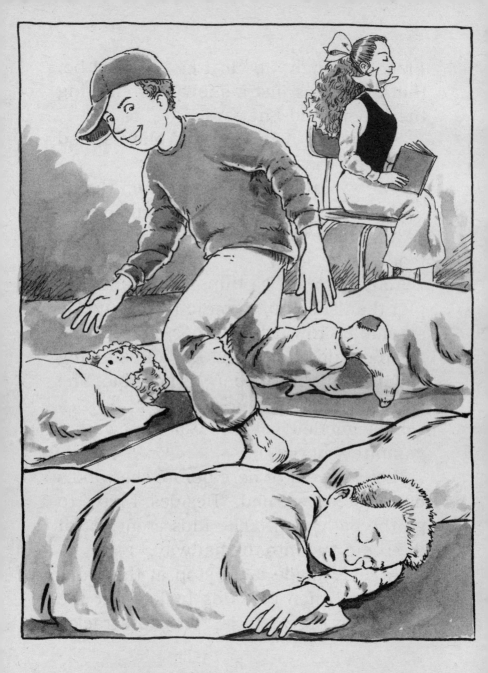

all right," Eddie said. "Or should I say, there WERE tracks."

The snow had been swept with what looked like a huge broom. "Probably workers trying to clear away snow so we can go home," Howie figured.

"You can see where they dumped paper or something, too," Melody said. She pointed to a few pieces of paper fluttering in the cold winter wind. The kids could feel the freezing air through the window.

Liza wasn't convinced. "Let's check out one more thing," she said. She led them through the hallway until they were at the door to the playground.

"Don't tell me you still think that snow dragon is alive and well," Melody said.

Eddie and Howie laughed. "Did the dragon borrow Frosty the Snowman's magic hat so it would come to life?" Eddie teased.

"Laugh all you want," Liza said. "But

when you're finished, you can explain where the dragon is NOW!"

Her friends looked out the window. Dr. Victor's yard was covered in mounds of snow, but there was nothing there that looked like a dragon.

"Maybe the storm knocked it down," Howie said after a moment of silence.

"Who cares about a dragon?" Eddie said. "Look at that!"

8

Winter Wonderland

"Wow!" Melody said. "It's beautiful!"

"It's an amusement park made entirely out of snow," Howie gasped.

"I can't wait to try it out!" Eddie shouted.

"What are you talking about?" Liza asked.

Eddie shoved her toward the window. "You were so busy looking for fairy-tale monsters, you missed seeing that!"

The playground had turned into a winter wonderland. Snow had drifted against the slide to form a giant snow cave. More snow had swirled against the swing set, making it look like an ice castle. Little scraps of paper fluttered over the pristine snow.

"Let's go get our coats!" Eddie said as

he raced back down the hall. Howie and Melody ran after him.

"What about the dragon?" Liza called.

Mrs. Jeepers' eyes flashed at the four kids when they skidded into the gym. A green-painted fingernail tapped on the green brooch at her throat. "Where have you four been?" she asked softly as kids woke up around her.

"I had to go to the bathroom," Melody said truthfully. "We didn't want to wake you up."

"Then we looked outside. We HAVE to go outside," Eddie told Mrs. Jeepers.

Melody nodded. "The playground is perfect for playing."

"Please let us. We can't stay cooped up inside until the snow melts," Howie added.

Kids all over the gym sat up and nodded. "We have hats!" somebody said.

"We have mittens!" Huey called out.

"We have boots," Carey told her teacher.

Kids jumped up and down and begged Mrs. Jeepers to let them go outside.

Finally, after conferring with Principal Davis, she agreed. The kids had milk and toast for breakfast and then they bundled up in coats, boots, hats, and gloves and raced out onto the playground.

"Heeeee-hah!" Eddie screamed when he slid down the snow slide. Kids ran all over the playground, checking out the snow creations. They added more snow to make the snow structures even bigger. Then they hollowed them out to make rooms and passageways.

"This is so cool," Melody said from inside the snow castle. She couldn't believe it had so many rooms.

Liza had to admit the playground was amazing, but she didn't feel like playing. She kept looking across the street at Dr. Victor's yard. Liza noticed that the snow in the scientist's yard wasn't white and smooth like the snow on the playground.

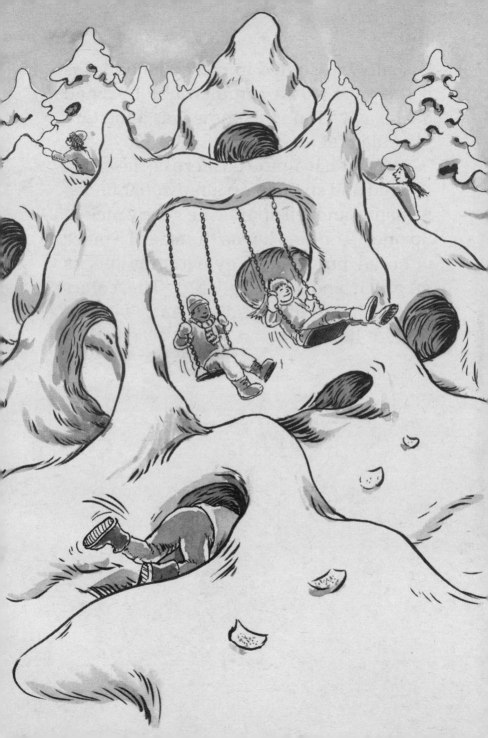

His snow was piled in messy mounds, as if the yard was a rumpled bed that had been slept in and the snow was a big tangled blanket.

Some trash fluttered across the playground and slapped up against her boots. It rustled and fell apart. She gently picked up one of the bits. It was the size of a piece of bread, but it was gray with tiny specks of green and blue and red. The colors caught in the dim sunlight and twinkled back at her.

"What's on that paper?" Melody panted as she kicked through the snow to see what Liza held.

"It isn't paper," Liza said, her eyes wide.

"Then what is it?" Melody asked.

Liza took a big breath before answering. "A dragon scale!"

Liza was sure Melody was going to make fun of her. Melody didn't get the chance. Just then a huge flash of light exploded from behind Dr. Victor's house. "Inside the school!" Mrs. Jeepers told the children.

"Run for your lives!" Liza screamed.

9

Dragon Potion

The kids raced into the safety of Bailey Elementary. Before the door slammed shut, Liza glanced over her shoulder. She was sure that she saw a huge shadow swoop over the playground.

"What was that?" kids wondered out loud.

Carey clutched Eddie's arm. "Did something explode?" she asked.

Eddie jerked his arm away. "It was just lightning," Eddie told her. He forgot to keep his voice down.

"In the winter?" Carey asked.

Eddie remembered what Howie had told them. "When the conditions are right, it can thunder in winter," he told her smugly.

Loud talking was never allowed in the halls. Mrs. Jeepers flashed her eyes at the kids. Everyone fell silent as she led them back to their classroom. "Please open your spelling books," Mrs. Jeepers told the kids once they'd put away their coats, boots, mittens, scarves, and gloves.

Eddie smacked his forehead. "I can't believe we're still trapped at school," he moaned. "Snow days usually mean we get to stay home. This is just WRONG! No kid should be forced to stay at school for twenty-four hours straight."

"What if we have to stay another night?" Carey asked, batting her eyelashes at Eddie.

Eddie was thinking about climbing out the windows and burrowing in the snow just to get away from Carey. Luckily for Eddie, Principal Davis's voice crackled over the loudspeaker. "Good morning to one and all," he said. "I am pleased to announce that the mayor plans for the city to reopen this afternoon. If all goes as scheduled, students should be able to go home at the regular time today."

As soon as Principal Davis stopped talking, the kids cheered. Even Mrs. Jeepers smiled an odd little half smile.

The only person that didn't seem happy was Liza. She sat quietly in her seat, peering out the window. She didn't talk after Mrs. Jeepers told them they could shut their books and stop working on math. Liza kept her mouth closed when Principal Davis let the entire school watch a movie in the middle of language arts time. She was even silent as the kids walked to the cafeteria for lunch.

"Are you okay?" Melody asked. "Do you have a fever?"

"Maybe you have snow sickness," Howie worried.

"Do you need to see the school nurse?" Eddie asked as the kids plopped their trays on the table in the corner.

Liza took a shaky breath. "No nurse can cure my problem," she said.

"What is it?" Eddie asked. "Chicken pox?"

Liza looked over her shoulder to make sure no one was listening. She had to talk in a whisper so Carey couldn't overhear.

"This is a problem bigger than chicken pox. I know what made those tracks around the school," she said.

"What?" Melody asked.

Liza gently pulled out what looked like a gray piece of paper from her pocket. "Whatever made those tracks left this behind," she said. "A dragon!"

Eddie laughed so hard, milk splurted out his nose. "Dragons aren't even real," he argued. "Forget about this fairy-tale monster."

"Dragons are just legends from the past," Howie agreed.

Liza shook her head. "Not anymore. I think Dr. Victor has cooked up a new concoction in his science lab." The kids were quiet. They believed the scientist

had once mixed a magic potion to make a Frankenstein monster.

"This time," Liza said, "he's made a dragon potion that brought the snow dragon to life."

The kids tried to reason with Liza. "But dragons aren't real," Melody repeated.

Liza argued right back. "Of course they're real. They used to hide treasures in caves. They once terrorized country-sides, burning fields with their fiery breath. Knights rode off to slay them. In fact, so many knights fought dragons that the dragons went into hiding. But now there's one flying around Bailey City."

"Even if what you're saying is true, why should we care?" Eddie wanted to know.

Liza looked Eddie in the eyes. "You, of all people, should care, because that very dragon beat the pants off you during a snowball fight."

Melody smiled. Howie grinned. But Eddie was not laughing.

"Dragons don't throw snowballs," Eddie told her.

"This one does," Liza said. "And there's something else they do."

"What?" her friends asked all at once.

Liza held up what they thought was the paper from the playground. Liza looked each of them in the eyes before answering. "They shed!"

10

Dragon's Lair

Howie gently took the scale from Liza to examine it.

"That's nothing but a scrap of paper," Eddie said.

Howie shook his head. "Liza may be on to something," he admitted. "This is no ordinary paper."

"Don't tell me you believe there's a dragon terrorizing our school too," Melody said with a tremor in her voice.

Howie nodded. "That's exactly what I think."

"If that's true, then where is your fantasy dragon now?" Eddie wanted to know.

Liza's forehead wrinkled with worry. "It escaped from Dr. Victor's yard for a reason. I think it's searching for something. The dragon won't rest until it finds it."

"This is the silliest thing I've ever heard," Eddie said. "That dragon didn't fly away. It just melted into a giant slush ball and I'll prove it."

Eddie jumped up from the table. He banged his tray on the side of the garbage can as he knocked off his scraps. "Follow me," Eddie told his friends as he headed out of the cafeteria. "Let's put this dragon tale to sleep once and for all."

"Where are we going?" Liza asked.

"To ride a dragon," Eddie teased.

"What?" Melody said in the hallway.

"If there is a dragon," Eddie said, "I want to have some fun."

"We can't just leave the school," Howie said, looking around to make sure no teachers were in the hallway.

"We won't go far," Eddie reasoned. "It'll just be for a few minutes."

Eddie and his three friends sneaked

back to the classroom. They slipped into their coats and boots, and then made their way to the playground door. The sun had finally broken through the clouds and the icicles hanging from the roof were dripping.

"Whatever you do," Liza said, "don't let Dr. Victor see us."

"Don't worry," Eddie said. "I bet Dr. Victor is stranded at the museum just like we've been stranded at school. We have nothing to worry about."

Liza kept glancing toward the sky as they made their way across the street and into Dr. Victor's backyard. She knew the strange flash of light had come from behind his house and she was scared. What if they really did see a dragon?

"This is too weird," Melody said slowly as the kids peeked into Dr. Victor's yard.

Howie gulped. The whole city looked like the North Pole except for Dr. Victor's backyard. There was absolutely no snow behind his house. All that was left was mud and some burned branches on a weeping willow tree. Giant tracks criss-crossed the yard as if a huge animal had been pacing in circles.

"Now you HAVE to believe me," Liza said. "I've just shown you the dragon's lair!"

Melody, Eddie, and Howie stared at the muddy yard. "What happened?" Melody gasped.

"The dragon melted all the snow with his fire breath," Liza said simply.

"Maybe we should call the police," Melody suggested.

"Or an exterminator," Eddie added.

"Exterminators are defenseless against dragons," Liza said. "And the police would never make it. The roads are still closed because of the snow."

"This could be a friendly dragon," Melody said hopefully. "Like the one in that song, 'Puff the Magic Dragon.'"

"Not this dragon," Liza said. "This dragon is mad."

"How do you know that?" Eddie asked. "Are you an expert in 'dragonology'?"

"Simple," Liza said. "When it was brought to life with Dr. Victor's magic potion, the dragon found nothing but frozen snow where its treasure should have been. Now it won't rest until it finds a treasure. A real treasure. WE have to find it for him before the rest of Bailey City ends up like Dr. Victor's backyard!"

11

1-800-Treasure

"Why don't we just call 1-800-Treasure?" Eddie suggested.

"I'm serious," Liza said.

Melody turned her nose up at the burnt smell in the backyard. "But we don't have any treasure to give a dragon."

"Even if I did have jewels and money, I'm not about to hand them over to a dragon with dandruff," Eddie said.

"Besides," Howie added, "we're stranded at school. We can't go looking for treasure."

"Then we'll have to find our treasure at Bailey Elementary," Liza said.

"Impossible," Eddie argued. "Schools don't have treasure. They don't even have enough money to buy good stuff."

"Or pay teachers what they deserve," Howie added.

"Schools do have something," Liza said. Then she told them her plan.

"You're nuts," Eddie said, shaking his head. Melody and Howie looked doubtful as they crept back into the school, but they didn't have a better idea, so they went to work during art class.

They went from kid to kid. "We're making a treasure box," Eddie lied. "Do you want to contribute?"

Carey batted her eyelashes at Eddie and gave him a pink plastic diamond ring. She talked her friends into putting in pennies, little books, photos, gel pens, and sticks of gum. Huey even had a piece of fool's gold in his pocket. Soon, they had Liza's pencil box filled.

Eddie, Melody, Howie, and Liza looked in the box. "This is no treasure," Eddie said, picking up a mini book.

"Of course it is," Liza said. "You can do

anything, go anywhere, or be anyone in a book."

"What about this?" Melody asked, picking up a class picture. "Mrs. Jeepers gave us this photo. She said all kids are treasures." Melody poked Eddie in the chest. "Even you!"

"What did you put in the box?" Howie asked Liza.

Liza held up a picture she had drawn of herself, Melody, Howie, and Eddie. "This

is our friendship," she said. "There's nothing more important than that."

Melody smiled. Howie patted Liza on the shoulder. Eddie blushed.

"But will the dragon think it's a treasure?" Howie asked.

Liza shrugged. "There's only one way to find out."

12

Real Treasure

The bell rang to end the school day. Eddie didn't walk out of school. He didn't run out of school. Eddie danced. He sang, "I'm going home, I've done my time. I get to play video games and eat candy until I puke."

Liza rolled her eyes. "What kind of song is that?" she asked.

"I thought you didn't like singing," Melody reminded him.

"This is the kind of song I like," Eddie admitted.

"But we have to do one thing first," Howie said, holding up the treasure box.

Eddie groaned. He'd already gone one whole afternoon without playing video games. He hated to wait any longer. Eddie sighed. "Let's do this crazy thing," he said.

Howie carried the cardboard box of treasures into Dr. Victor's backyard.

"Put it right by that willow tree," Liza suggested.

"Now we just have to wait and see what happens," Melody said.

"You guys can wait," Eddie said. "I'm going home. I bet my grandmother misses me."

"I miss my mom," Liza said softly. Secretly, she was eager to leave Dr. Victor's backyard, too. Being in a dragon's lair made her shiver. "I guess we can check on the treasure tomorrow."

The four kids raced to their own houses, eager to see their families.

The next morning, the sun shone warm and bright. Icicles dripped and a snowplow cleared the street by the school. Melody, Liza, Howie, and Eddie met in front of Dr. Victor's house.

"Have you checked the backyard?" Eddie asked. He was the last one to arrive and still had a chocolate milk mustache from breakfast.

"No," Liza said, "but I heard a *whomp-whomp-swoosh* sound last night. That dragon was flying overhead."

"I woke up early this morning," Melody reported. "I heard the strangest thing. It wasn't a thump. It sounded more like a really big cat purring."

"We're sitting ducks out here for a hungry dragon." Liza shaded her eyes from the bright sun and looked at Dr. Victor's house.

"I don't think we have to worry," Howie said as he pointed. Their treasure box was sitting on the curb. It was a little singed around the edges, but it was empty.

"Oh, my gosh. It worked," Melody said.

"The dragon liked our treasures," Howie added.

"Silly dragon," Eddie said. "He didn't

know the difference between a real treasure and a fake one."

"Maybe," Liza said as she patted Eddie
on his back, "the dragon just needed a
hint about what REALLY matters."

About the Authors

Debbie Dadey and Marcia Thornton Jones have fun writing stories together. When they both worked at an elementary school in Lexington, Kentucky, Debbie was the school librarian and Marcia was a teacher. During their lunch break in the school cafeteria, they came up with the idea of the Bailey School Kids.

Debbie and her family live in Fort Collins, Colorado. Marcia and her husband live in Kentucky. How do these authors write together? They talk on the phone and use computers and fax machines!

Learn more about Debbie and Marcia at their Web site, www.BaileyKids.com!